For my grandparents

The Little Matchstick Girl

Based on the story by Hans Christian Andersen
Illustrated by Debbie Lavreys

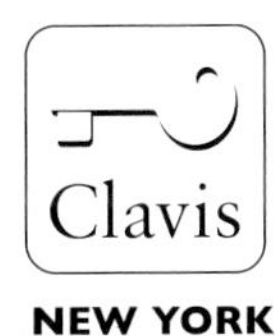

Clavis
NEW YORK

Once upon a time, there was a poor little girl who wandered around all alone on New Year's Eve. It had been snowing all day and now night was beginning to fall; there was a sharp chill in the air. The girl was so poor that she didn't even have shoes, and only a shabby coat to keep her warm. In the pocket, were her matches.

The girl tried to sell the matches to earn money. She approached everyone she saw, but she hadn't sold a single stick yet. The people only gave her a strange look and walked on. How cold and hungry she was! The girl looked in the windows of the houses she passed. Inside it was warm and she could smell goose roasting in the oven. Outside the snowflakes fell on her fair, blond hair.

Tired, the girl sat down in front of a house. She drew in her legs to warm her feet, but after a few minutes she was shivering even more than before. She had to keep moving to stay warm. She still had a pocket full of matches and no money to give her father. She didn't dare to return home. There, her father was waiting for her in an old shack where the cold wind blew in through the broken windows.

The girl's hands were almost frozen. Perhaps she should light just one match to warm herself with? She hesitated, but then took a match out of her pocket. Hsss. It blazed up and burned fiercely. When the girl looked up, she saw a stove glowing warmly. But as soon as she stretched out her legs to warm her feet, the flame went out. When she looked up again, the stove was gone.

The girl lit a second match. Immediately, a bright light fell on the wall behind her. It became a warm and cozy dining room. The table was set with the finest china she had ever seen. There were dishes full of food and in the middle was a large platter with a roasted goose. She could almost taste it. But then the flame went out and all she saw was the snow covered wall.

Should she light a third match? What she had seen when she had lit the other two matches had been so magnificent. Quickly, she lit a third match before she could think the better of it. All of a sudden, she was sitting under the biggest Christmas tree she had ever seen. Its branches were long and green and it was decorated with colorful ornaments and sparkling lights. Cautiously, the girl tried to touch one of the ornaments, but then the flame of the third match went out and the Christmas tree vanished.

Three charred matches lay next to the girl – and she still wasn't warm. Night had fallen, the moon was high in the sky and a thousand stars were shining. Just then, a falling star shot across the night sky. Someone just went to heaven, the girl thought. That was what her grandma used to say. Her grandma who used to take her in her lap and tell her stories. But that was a long time ago; now her grandma was in heaven.

The girl couldn't resist lighting a fourth match. What would she see this time, she wondered. Her grandma appeared. With open arms and a warm smile, she stepped through a gate.

"My sweet grandma," the girl cried, "please take me with you to heaven, for I know you will be gone when the flame goes out and I can't bear for you to disappear like the warm stove, the roasted goose, and the sparkling Christmas tree."

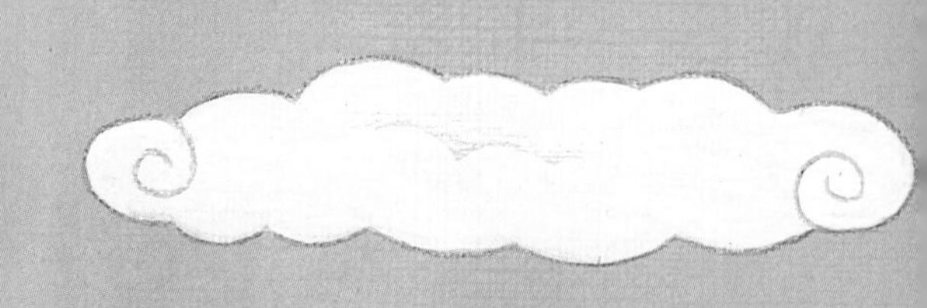

Quickly, the girl lit all the matches that remained in her pocket. She wanted to be with her grandma forever. How tall and beautiful her grandma looked in the bright light. She took the girl in her arms and together they went to heaven. High above the earth, the girl no longer suffered from cold and hunger. She was now close to the clouds, the stars, and the moon.

The next morning, the girl was found laying silently in the snow. Forever asleep. Her cheeks were red and she was smiling. All around her were charred matches. "She wanted to warm herself," the people who found her there said. But no one knew the magnificent things she had seen, nor how glad she was to start the new year with her grandma – how happy she was to be in heaven.

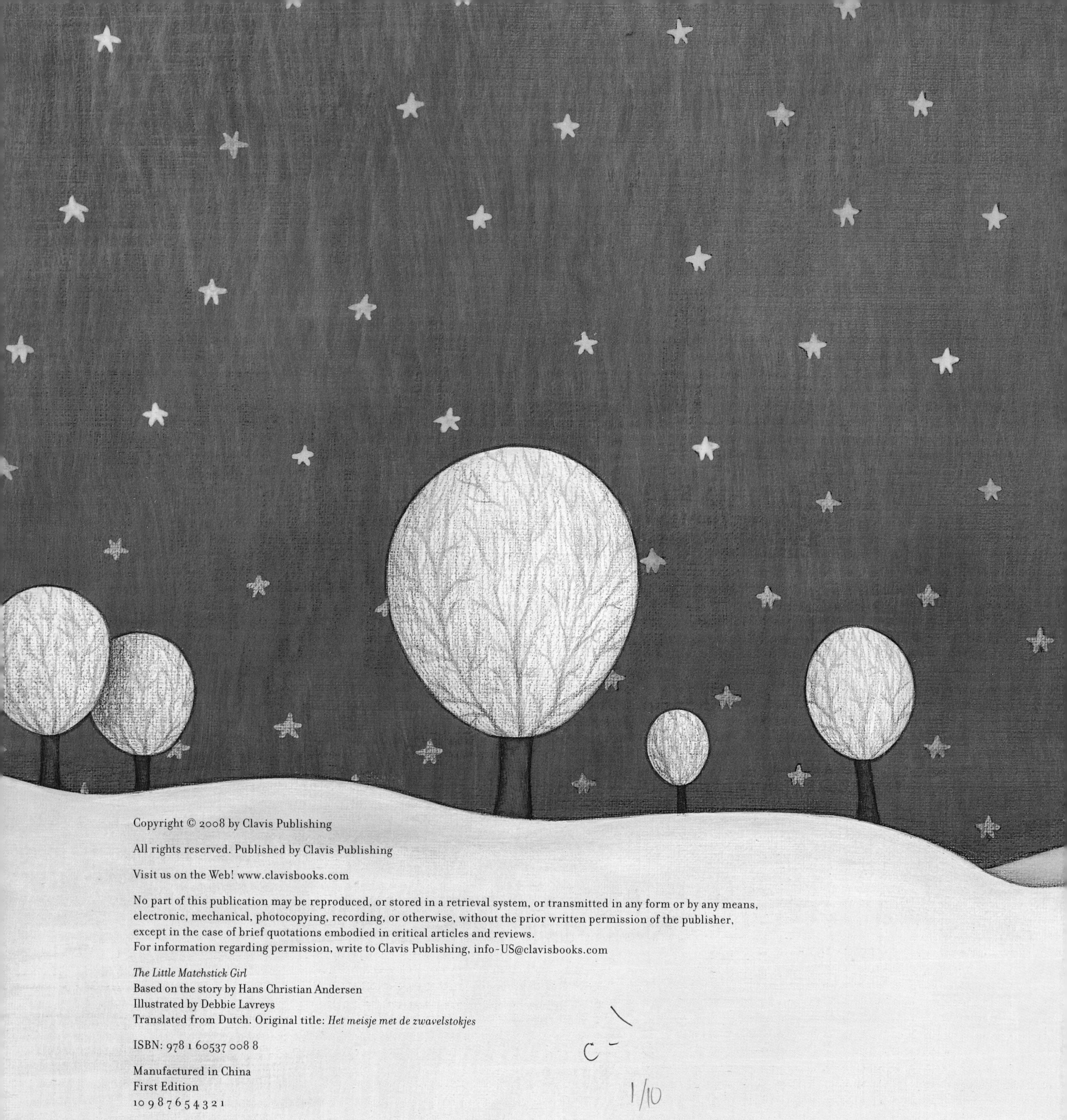

Visit us on the Web! www.clavisbooks.com

The Little Matchstick Girl
Based on the story by Hans Christian Andersen
Illustrated by Debbie Lavreys
Translated from Dutch. Original title: *Het meisje met de zwavelstokjes*

ISBN: 978 1 60537 008 8

Manufactured in China
First Edition
10 9 8 7 6 5 4 3 2 1

Clavis Publishing supports the First Amendment and celebrates the right to read.